WEIRD
SPORTS
OF THE
WORLD

By S.B. Watson

The Child's World

Published by The Child's World®
1980 Lookout Drive
Mankato, MN 56003-1705
800-599-READ
www.childsworld.com

The Child's World®: Mary Berendes, Publishing Director
The Design Lab: Design and production

Photo credits
Cover: iStock (left); Bill Stevenson/World of Stock (right)
Interior: AP/Wide World: 6, 13, 14; Corbis: 22;
dreamstime.com: 8, 10; iStock: 5, 21; Jun Tanlayco: 17;
Bill Stevenson/World of Stock: 18.

Library of Congress Cataloging-in-Publication Data
Watson, S. B., 1953–
 Weird sports of the world / by S.B. Watson.
     p. cm.
 Includes bibliographical references and index.
 ISBN 978-1-60954-378-5 (library bound: alk. paper)
 1. Sports—Juvenile literature. 2. Curiosities and wonders—
Juvenile literature. I. Title.
 GV705.4.W38 2011
 796–dc22   2010042901

Printed in the United States of America
Mankato, Minnesota
September, 2011
PA02108

*Above: Hockey without
ice . . . on one wheel!
See page 16 to find
out more!*

*For more information
about the photo on
page 1, turn to page 8.*

TABLE OF CONTENTS

For more news about off-road skateboarding, head to page 18!

The Weird, Weird World of Sports

Everywhere in the world, people love sports. Some sports are games you'll know. Some you might even play yourself, such as baseball, football, or soccer. But then there are the "other" sports, the ones you don't see on TV or the playground. These are the *weird* sports of the world. We'll be looking at a bunch in this book. So hold your breath, grab your chess-boxing gloves, point your kayak to the edge of a waterfall, and get ready for action!

No matter where you go around the world, people love to play sports!

FAST FACT!

Some of the sports in this book can be dangerous. Please don't try them yourself without help from an adult.

5

The player in white is holding his breath and trying to tag his opponents. The players in blue are trying to stop him!

Kabaddi, Kabaddi, Kabbadi!

Kabaddi is a game played in India and Southeast Asia. Two teams of seven players stand on a small court. It's divided into halves. Each team takes a turn sending one player into the other team's half. His or her job is to tag as many opponents as possible and return to the other side of the court. Now . . . here's the weird part. The player must do all this on only one breath! To prove that he or she is not breathing, the player must chant the word "kabaddi" over and over without pausing to breathe. The action can get rough, but no one loses their breath!

Who Needs Ladders?

You might have played this weird French-African sport without even knowing it. Have you ever run a race through an **obstacle** course? Have you ever raced through your neighborhood jumping over fences? Take that to the extreme and you've got Parkour. In this sport, players run, climb, and jump as smoothly as possible over obstacles. These can include fences, walls, rocks, tree branches, or buildings. Players flip and twist around objects, too. Experts do Parkour in cities such as London and Paris, too. They leap from walls, buildings, and rooftops. Yikes!

Parkour moves combine gymnastics with bravery, such as this one-handed handstand.

FAST FACT!

Here are some popular Parkour moves:
- **The Pop Vault (using a wall to lift yourself higher into the air)**
- **The Cat Jump (diving over an object and then tucking your legs in to clear it)**
- **The Underbar (jumping or swinging through the air)**

Look out below! The Elfego Baca course tees off from the top of a mountain like this one.

A Loooong Way to the Green!

Who ever heard of a golf **tournament** with only one hole? If that hole starts on the top of a mountain—one is more than enough! At the Elfego Baca Golf Shoot in Socorro, Mexico, golfers start on Socorro Peak. They tee off from a height of 7,280 feet (2,219 meters). The hole is 2 ½ miles (4 km) below! Golfers bring friends to help find their golf balls on the rocky ground. It can take 9 to 15 shots—and several hours!—to cover the rugged distance.

Who Needs a Car?

First introduced in Finland, wife-carrying is just what it says. A man carries a female teammate (usually his wife, but sometimes just a friend). Then they race! They run on a special obstacle course. The obstacles include cold pools of water, hurdles, and rope swings. Types of carries include piggyback or the fireman's carry (over the shoulder). The most popular style was invented in Estonia. The woman hangs upside-down with her legs around the husband's shoulders. She holds onto his waist with her arms.

For this part of the course, the woman has to try to keep her head out of the water!

In the Estonian carry, the women can't always see where the team is going. The ladies might wear helmets in case they get dropped!

13

WEIRD FACT!

As if running through fire pits and barbed wire wasn't enough . . . the race is always held in the freezing January weather!

It Takes a Tough Guy to Win

Most athletes are pretty tough people. Football players get whacked by lineman. **Marathon** runners fight through a 26-mile (42-km) race. Hockey players get slammed into the boards. But that's nothing compared to our next sport! The runners in the Tough Guy Race in England live up to their name. First, there's a long foot race. After the foot race, the obstacle course begins. Runners must race through underwater tunnels and fire pits. They climb over (or under) electric fences and barbed wire. They have to burst through patches of sharp-thorned **nettles**. They end up muddy, tired, and cold—but happy!

After braving a chilly pond, this runner has to leap over flaming weeds!

Flat Tires in Hockey?

The **forward** uses his stick to control the ball. He speeds toward the goal. Spotting an open player ahead, he fires a pass. But the pass is **intercepted**, and the two teams race back the other way. The **center** shoots. The goalie tries to block the shot, but the ball trickles past him. It's a goal! Sounds like hockey, right? Well it is—except that the players are riding unicycles! In unicycle hockey, players ride the one-wheeled bikes while using hockey sticks to hit a ball. Unicycle hockey is played in Europe, Australia, and New Zealand, as well as the United States.

Here's some stick-swinging action from a unicycle hockey game in New Zealand!

WEIRD FACT!

Unicycle hockey has been around as a sport since the 1960s. But a German film from 1925 shows two unicyclists with hockey sticks chasing a ball!

FAST FACT!

Mountain boarding is also known as dirt boarding, off-road boarding, grass boarding, and all-terrain boarding.

Off-road Boarding

You climb on your board and speed down the mountain. You're cutting left and right, carving great turns. Suddenly, your wheel hits a rock. Why would your snowboard have a wheel? Because this isn't snowboarding, it's mountain boarding! This sport combines skateboarding and snowboarding, but with no snow. Mountain boarders use oversized skateboards with large rubber wheels. The sport started in Australia. It's also popular in England and the United States. It blends the speed and skill of snowboarding with the danger of off-road sports. Don't forget helmets, knee pads, and elbow pads!

Mountain boarders wear a lot of gear to protect them in case they fall.

Look Out Below!

This may be the most dangerous of all our weird world sports. Athletes paddle their kayaks to the edge of a tall waterfall—then they keep going! The kayak plunges over the waterfall toward the raging river below. The kayaker must remain in the kayak all the way down. After the kayak lands, he or she keeps paddling. Popular waterfalls for kayakers include Spain's Sauth deth Pish falls and Brazil's Salto Belo falls.

This kayaker is ready for a hard landing in the pool below!

FAST FACT!

The world waterfall kayaking record is held by American Tyler Bradt. He went over a 186-foot (57-m) waterfall in Washington!

First, I'll move this pawn . . . then I'll get up and bonk you on the nose.

Uppercut . . . and Checkmate!

You usually don't think about boxing and chess together. That is, until you read about chess boxing, a combination of brains and **brawn**. Two players meet in a boxing ring and fight for three minutes. Then they take off their gloves . . . and play chess! After a few minutes, it's back to boxing, then back to chess. That goes back-and-forth for eleven rounds or until there's a knockout—or a checkmate!

Glossary

brawn—physical strength

center—in hockey, the player at the middle of the front line

forward—in hockey, the position farthest from his own goal

Hindi—a language spoken in India

intercepted—in football, when a pass is caught by the defense instead of the offense

marathon—a running race that covers 26 miles, 385 yards (42.2 km)

nettle—a plant that has sharp thorns on it

obstacle—barrier; something blocking your way.

tournament—competition

Web Sites

For links to learn more about weird sports: **childsworld.com/links**

Note to Parents, Teachers, and Librarians: We routinely verify our Web links to make sure they are safe and active sites. So encourage your readers to check them out!

Index